This book belongs to:

. . . .

. . . .

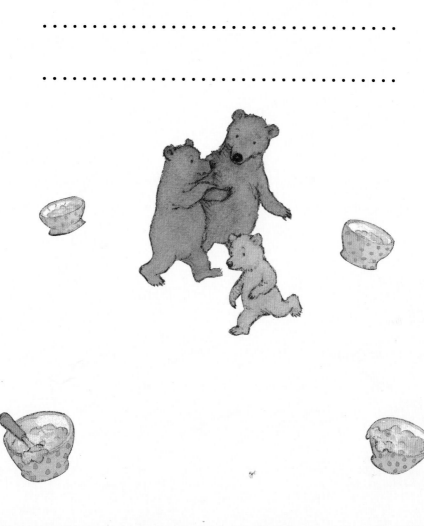

Retold by Sue Graves
Illustrated by Priscilla Lamont

Reading consultants: Betty Root and Monica Hughes

Marks and Spencer p.l.c.
PO Box 3339
Chester, CH99 9QS

shop online
www.marksandspencer.com

ISBN 978-1-84461-584-1
Printed in China

First Readers

Read Together

Goldilocks
and the
Three Bears

MARKS &
SPENCER

Helping your child to read

First Readers are closely linked to the National Curriculum. Their vocabulary has been carefully selected from the word lists recommended by the National Literacy Strategy.

Read the story

Read the story
to your child
a few times.

That morning, a little girl was walking in the woods.
Her name was Goldilocks.
She saw the three bears' cottage.
"What a pretty cottage!" she said.
"I'll look inside."
Goldilocks went in.

12

Follow your finger

Run your finger under
the text as you read.
Your child will soon begin to
follow the words with you.

Look at the pictures
Talk about the pictures. They will help your child to understand the story.

Goldilocks went in.

13

Have a go
Let your child have a go at reading the large type on each right-hand page. It repeats a line from the story.

Join in
When your child is ready, encourage them to join in with the main story text. Shared reading is the first step to reading alone.

Once there were three bears.
There was Daddy Bear, Mummy Bear
and Baby Bear.
They lived in a cottage in the woods.

Once there were three bears.

One morning, Mummy Bear made
some hot porridge.
"Let's go for a walk while it cools," said
Daddy Bear.
So the three bears went out.

The three bears went out.

That morning, a little girl was walking in the woods.

Her name was Goldilocks.

She saw the three bears' cottage.

"What a pretty cottage!" she said.

"I'll look inside."

Goldilocks went in.

Goldilocks went in.

Goldilocks saw three bowls of porridge.
She felt hungry so she tried some.
But Daddy Bear's porridge was
too hot.
Mummy Bear's porridge was too cold.
Then she tried Baby Bear's porridge.
The porridge was just right.
Goldilocks ate it all up!

The porridge was just right.

Then Goldilocks saw three chairs.
She felt tired so she sat down.
But Daddy Bear's chair was too hard.
Mummy Bear's chair was too soft.
Then she tried Baby Bear's chair.
The chair was just right.
But Goldilocks broke it!

The chair was just right.

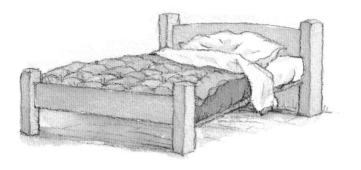

Goldilocks went upstairs.

She saw three beds.

She felt sleepy so she lay down.

But Daddy Bear's bed was too wide.

Mummy Bear's bed was too long.

Then she tried Baby Bear's bed.

The bed was just right.

Goldilocks fell asleep!

The bed was just right.

Then the three bears came back.
They looked at their porridge.
"Who's been eating my porridge?"
said Daddy Bear.
"Who's been eating my porridge?"
said Mummy Bear.
"Who's been eating my porridge?"
said Baby Bear. "And eaten it up!"

"Who's been eating
my porridge?"

The three bears looked at their chairs.
"Who's been sitting in my chair?" said
Daddy Bear.
"Who's been sitting in my chair?" said
Mummy Bear.
"Who's been sitting in my chair?" said
Baby Bear. "And broken it!'

"Who's been sitting in
my chair?"

The three bears went upstairs.
They looked at their beds.
"Who's been sleeping in my bed?" said
Daddy Bear.
"Who's been sleeping in my bed?" said
Mummy Bear.
"Who is sleeping in my bed?" said
Baby Bear. "She's still there!"

"Who is sleeping in my bed?"

Suddenly, Goldilocks woke up.
She saw the three bears.
They looked very cross.
Goldilocks ran away.
And the three bears never saw
her again!

Goldilocks ran away.

Look back in your book.
Can you read these words?

Daddy Bear

Mummy Bear

porridge

Baby Bear

Goldilocks

28

Can you answer these questions?

What did Mummy
Bear make?

What happened
to Baby Bear's
chair?

Where did the
bears find
Goldilocks?

Read Together

Look out for other books in the **First Readers** range
(subject to availability):

Fairytale Readers